Submitting to the Dominatrix

A Cuckold's Sexual Awakening Part 2

Amber Carden

Chapter 1: The Second Invitation 3

Chapter 2: A Special Gift 23

Chapter 3: Pushing Boundaries 37

Chapter 4: Redefining Boundaries 52

Chapter 5: The Edge of Ecstasy 61

Chapter 1: The Second Invitation

Ethan

I used to pride myself on knowing my wife Ava's body better than anyone. The way she would arch into me, her breath hitching, nails digging into my skin.

It all disintegrated when she moaned another man's name while I was inside her.

"Harder, Jax."

I went soft mid-thrust, the weight of her words crushing any connection I thought we had left. Her voice whispering another man's name, unraveling the tight balance inside. How long had I been a stranger in my own bed?

Even now, when I close my eyes, those words echo. A whispered taunt.

"Harder, Jax."

I tighten my grip around the steering wheel and exhale, staring at the traffic.

I haven't been able to hold an erection since.

It's been three blasted weeks.

"It was a stupid mistake. You make it feel like it was deliberate."

"Can we please stop dragging this out? I miss my husband."

"I'm trying here, Eth, but you keep pulling away. What else am I supposed to do?"

Her passive-aggressive tone is a haunting reminder of my parents' marriage.

I feel trapped in a loop, waking up covered in sweat from dreams of my father storming into my room after fights with Mom. The suffocation I felt then is stronger than ever.

I shake it off as my phone vibrates on the dashboard. My wife's name flashes on the screen.

"Have you left work?"

I've barely opened the text when the message disappears. Another one asks: *"Should I get the beef from the freezer for hamburgers tonight?"*

I lock my screen and put my phone away, pulling out of the parking lot. Turning on the radio, I switch between channels until I catch some rock music. Guns N' Roses might lift my spirits.

I don't even notice when I start singing along. But as I spot the gym's signage, I switch gears and decide to head home instead.

I need to fix things with Ava. Avoiding each other has to end.

The huge sports bike parked right outside our porch has me killing the loud 'Sweet Child O' Mine'. My gut instantly warns me I'm not going to like what I find inside.

I leave the car by the road and walk in slowly, each of the last twenty steps feeling like a minefield.

I don't hear any moans like I had suspected. Just the sound of skin slapping. Rapid. Hard.

My head fills with images when I hear a muffled sound.

The first thing I see right from the door is a naked man– tattooed sleeve arms, pierced ears, shorn hair, bearded face.

Positioned behind my wife, holding tight to the silk scarf stuffed inside her mouth, he pistons in and out of her, gritting his teeth, grunting like an animal.

Despite her body straining awkwardly over the couch, the way Ava arches into him, meeting his thrusts, makes it clear—this isn't forced. She is enjoying this.

While the slapping sounds continue, I take in the scene: his leather jacket on the floor, her discarded bra, and torn panties. The framed wedding photo on the wall feels like a slap, forcing me to back up.

I want to scream, but I steady my breathing. This has to be a sick joke.

Ava's eyes are tightly shut so she misses my entry but as my phone slips out of my grip and drops to the floor, their steady momentum breaks.

The shattering sound has her eyes fly open.

For a moment, she looks caught, her mouth forming a silent 'oh' as the man continues thrusting into her. But then, with a shuddering breath, she arches into him once more, her body betraying any remorse she might have had.

In the next beat, she lets out a strangled cry. Her mouth opens wider, her nails digging hard into the cushions and her head thrown back in pleasure.

The skinhead, finally registering my presence, pulls out of her–letting the scarf drop.

I get a clear view of his glistening cock, coated in her juices, without a condom.

This is what we've come down to.

The last unbroken rules of our open marriage of not bringing dates home and always using protection — now broken.

He palms his length, eyes narrowed at me, a hint of irritation in them.

He didn't finish and is waiting for me to leave so he can continue screwing my wife in my home.

Grabbing my phone from the floor, I walk out and get behind the wheel, driving blindly.

The burn inside me growing.

It's a full ten minutes after which my phone starts to ring but I ignore it.

Of course, it's my wife. She waited for her fling to finish and leave before even thinking of me.

I suddenly understand the reason Ava was messaging earlier. She just wanted to know what time I was getting home. Was it going to be a quickie or could she let the man take his time on her? That's all she wanted to know.

I drive to the nearest hotel, get a room, and leaving my phone and the jacket in the room, head straight to the rooftop bar. I don't want to be alone.

The cool breeze from the rooftop bar should be soothing, but it only makes the ache worse. I take a seat at the farthest corner of the bar, order a drink, and try to drown out the buzz inside my head.

The amber liquid does little to pull the image of my wife getting fucked by who I can only assume is Jax.

Ava truly has me cuckolded.

Maybe agreeing to open this marriage was a mistake. But I don't think closing it again will do anything now.

The thought of ending it enters my head, but how do I move away from ten years together? She has stayed with me through my worst. My accident, losing jobs, my mood swings. She fought for me—stood up to my father, worked extra shifts when I started my firm.

How do I turn my back on all that?

But then my mind throws the picture of Jax fucking her raw and her letting go right in front of my eyes.

I clench my jaw and do a quick bottoms-up before asking for a repeat.

The bar starts filling up, but I barely notice until someone slides onto the chair next to me. A woman. Her floral perfume is delicate but insistent. I don't look up. I can feel her eyes on me though.

"Rough night?"

Not wanting to engage, I leave her effort unanswered. The silence stretches. But when she doesn't push, I glance at her.

Light hair, dark eyes, face scrubbed clean. Her dress seems to be her only effort before getting here. It's short, racy, black and it highlights her best feature–her gigantic tits.

She smiles. "That bad, huh?"

"I've had worse," I lie, taking a swig from my drink, feeling the burn down my throat.

She turns in her seat, facing me fully now. Her eyes filled with curiosity. "You look like you want to punch something, but don't know where to start."

"Yeah, well... there's a lot to punch."

She raises an eyebrow before leaning in just slightly, enough to show she's interested. Her tits squished together in the process.

"I get it," she whispers. "For me, it's always the ones closest to you that do the worst."

I stare at her, my throat tight. Something about her words gets to me- cuts deeper than the drinks have managed to.

"Yeah?" I ask, my voice lower. "Lose anyone precious?"

She looks down at her glass, the hint of a smile fading. "Only someone I thought I couldn't bear to live without." She takes a swig and her lips curl. "It's crazy how quickly the haze clears up after a bit of distraction."

For the first time in weeks, I feel something other than hollowness or dull ache in me. I feel seen.

Suddenly I'm interested, but she leaves before I can respond, disappearing into the crowd.

I try to follow her movement for a while but give up. Maybe it's best this way.

I finish my drink and decide to head back. As I'm making my way through the crowd, I catch a glimpse of her again. She's talking to someone else, but her eyes keep flitting back to me, igniting a spark within.

I take a deep breath and just as our eyes meet, I gesture my head toward the door, a subtle hint of invitation.

She follows, her steps hesitant yet purposeful.

As we step out of the door, I feel an arm slide through mine. The familiar floral scent hits me, and I can't help but smile. "I was hoping you'd come."

"I wasn't sure you had game," she replies, a playful smirk playing on her lips. "But hey!" she says, shrugging her shoulders, "we need to take our chances."

That makes me laugh, a rush of excitement coursing through me.

She presses the button to the penthouse, and we both remain silent till we're inside her room.

The moment the door shuts, her lips find mine and I lose myself in the distraction, the taste of her an escape from the chaos inside my head.

Her fingers furiously working on the buttons of my shirt, and mine pushing the straps of her dress down her shoulders.

Her lips are frantic, as we stumble toward the bed. Her ample tits press against my chest as we both hurry to get our clothes off while still kissing.

By the time we hit the mattress, our clothes are all gone, and I'm only in my boxers. She straddles me, her hands slipping under the waistband, and for the first time in weeks, I feel alive—hard, ready.

Her fingers are rough and her movements are slightly aggressive but that only gets me harder.

She giggles leaning in to kiss my neck, her warm breath tickling my skin. My cock rubs against her stomach as I twirl her nipples between my fingers, pulling more moans from her.

I can feel the slickness of her slit on my thigh. As she moans again, I'm suddenly reminded of Ava and my insides deflate.

"Do you want me to take charge?" she whispers, her voice thick with excitement.

"I don't mind," I reply distracted, trying to focus on the feel of her skin.

She blinks but doesn't question my detachment, her need to be in control taking over.

She reaches into the headboard's niche, pulling out a condom, and I inhale sharply as she rolls it down over my length, the sensation electrifying.

"You're thick," she murmurs, biting her lip as her fingers glide over me. My body tenses, the pulse in my veins racing.

"As long as you're okay with it," I rasp, wanting to stay in the moment.

She positions herself over me, and I watch her through half-lidded eyes. The bright lights in the room leave nothing to the imagination. Her skin isn't flawless. There's a scar on her stomach, her breasts sagging a little.

But none of that matters. I don't care about her imperfections.

She lowers herself onto me, and I close my eyes.

I just want to feel something.

The heat of her surrounds me, and I grit my teeth, pushing up deeper into her. She gasps as she takes all of me in. Her nails dig into my chest as she stills, adjusting to the stretch of me inside her.

I notice her eyes watering and I rub her thighs, letting her get comfortable with my girth.

"Fuck! I need a moment," she breathes out.

I distract her by reaching between her legs, slowly teasing her clit, rubbing my thumb over it in circles and she moans before starting to move.

I fondle her tits as she slowly starts picking up pace.

The wet warmth, the tightness, and the friction feel great. I bite back a groan, letting the woman above me set the pace, her moans filling the room as she starts riding me.

My fingers dig into her hips as she grinds harder, and I can feel her clenching around me, her body trembling as she edges closer.

Her nails drag across my chest, a sharp sting mixed with the overwhelming pleasure, and I gasp, my control slipping. My mind flashes to Dove, the way her nails would rake down my nipples, sending jolts of electricity through me.

My cock throbs at the memory, and I focus solely on the pleasure, letting it take over.

Holding her firm in her place, I start thrusting up into her, harder, deeper, and her moans turn into desperate cries as she shatters all over my cock.

I let out a low grunt as she clenches around me and unable to hold back anymore, I pick up pace till suddenly my vision goes white and I halt all movement.

She starts moving over me, drawing out my pleasure, milking my cock and I have to grit my teeth to keep myself from screaming.

"Fuck, Dove!"

While the stranger collapses onto my chest, panting and trembling, I don't move. I don't open my eyes, either, letting myself pretend, just for a second longer that it's Dove that just came all over my cock.

But the illusion crumbles as I inhale her scent.

As soon as she slips off to the bathroom, I hop out of bed, pulling my clothes on with practiced speed, my mind already miles away.

The bathroom door clicks shut, and I head for the door, my hand resting on the knob when her voice stops me.

"Hey! I never got your name," she calls out, her voice soft, teasing.

I turn, offering a polite smile, and she giggles, sensing my hesitation. "It's okay. I'll file you in my head as John Doe."

I smile, but it's hollow, and with one last glance, I leave.

The shrill sound of my ringing phone greets me when I step back in my hotel room.

Has to be Ava.

Ignoring it, I head to the bathroom. A long, hot shower relaxes my muscles, but the images of Ava and the stranger still claw at my thoughts. I try to push them away, focusing instead on the warm water and the hum of the ventilation fan.

When I return to the room, the damned thing is still ringing. Slamming the door behind me, I check the screen to find multiple texts.

"Eth, I'm really sorry about today. I know I shouldn't have brought anyone home."

"Can we please talk? At least come home. I'm worried about you."

"Please, Ethan. I'm desperate to fix this. Can we at least talk?"

I blankly stare at it for a while as my jaw tightens before tossing it back on the table.

It buzzes a few times more and I check the damned thing again.

The desperation in her texts makes my heart clench. I'm oscillating between wanting to soothe her and hurting her.

The three dots appear again. She's typing something so I draft a scathing one from my end.

"You made your bed. Now I need to think about the next steps."

I hit send, feeling a grim satisfaction but her text arrives the next second.

"Leon's Grotto is hosting another meet-up next week. They just sent an invite... but we don't have to go if you don't want to."

I stare at the words, my mind racing. I know I need to confront Ava and settle our mess, but the allure of another night at Leon's Grotto is too strong to ignore. The chance to see Dove again—an escape from the chaos—is something I can't pass up. Especially now.

Maybe this will bring the clarity I need.

Chapter 2: A Special Gift

Ethan

"Babe, could you pass the water?"

Ava's casual tone, the way she slings 'Babe' like a badge of intimacy from behind the wheel, makes me want to roll down her window and shove her head out for a solid minute.

The relentless August rain could probably quench her thirst.

Instead, I unclip my seatbelt, reach into the back seat, and toss the bottle into her lap without saying a word. My gaze shifts to the lush green stretch outside as I clip my belt back on.

The sky, once bright and blue, has turned grey–like a switch flipped somewhere between our small talk and silence. I'm stuck here, in this confined space, with my wife, heading to a jungle resort for our second "experience" with Leon's Grotto.

"There are a few cafes up ahead if you want to stop for something hot," Ava chirps, her voice unnervingly upbeat.

I grab a bag of chips from the glove box, turn on the radio, and stare out the window.

She sighs, her fingers brushing my arm, but I pretend not to notice. Her touch feels forced—like she's trying too hard to keep something alive.

As we wind through the road to Catskills, the vivid fall foliage blurs by, and all I can think about is Dove.

Her voice. Her scent. Her control.

But what about Julien?

She is his submissive. I'm just their one-time trophy. So why has he invited us back? What's really going on?

Hoping for clues, or maybe just a glimpse of Dove, I staked out their gallery, D'Armonde Muse, twice after we got the second invite. Got nothing. Only the creepy feeling of being followed back to Westchester each time.

My mind has thrown a few possibilities at me.

Maybe Dove is leveling up in her Dominatrix training, and I'd be their tool—again.

Maybe Julien has found someone new for her, and we're just there to indulge with everyone else.

Or maybe this is a trap.

The rational part of me keeps throwing logic at the situation, but all I can hear is Dove's whisper to Julien: *"What if we keep him?"*

I'm smiling like an idiot at that reminder as we enter the gates of the resort.

Maybe Dove asked for me as a reward. I have four days to find out.

Ava flicks the car lock just as I'm about to step out and I frown.

The thought of seeing her again heats my blood. But then, Ava's fingers tighten around my wrist, dragging me back into the present, back into this car with her.

"I don't want to go in if you're not even going to talk to me." She locks the door just as I'm about to get out, her voice trembling. A hint of desperation in it. "I feel so fucking alone."

I clench my jaw and slump back in my seat. "I'm angry," I say, the words coming out sharper than I intended.

"Then do something about it," she whispers. "Show me. Scream at me. Hurt me."

Her lips part slightly, and I feel the tension snap between us. My body tightens in response. Damn her for knowing exactly what buttons to push.

Her voice lowers an octave, taking on a sultry tone. "If it helps, make me watch… you with others. Maybe that's what we need."

She thinks it's easy. I know it would hurt. It's why I never told her about Dove or any of the other women I've fucked.

My gaze locks with hers, and for a moment, all the hurt and anger melts into something more primal. Something I can't fight off. She's challenging me, and I hate that it's working.

She leans in and crashes her lips on mine for a brief kiss. Ten seconds maybe and whispers, "I'm still yours," before pulling away.

I let out a little hum and nod.

We leave everything in the car, and as we approach the front desk, I wrap my arm around her shoulder, pulling her closer.

The setting sun casts a warm glow over the resort, where individual cottages dot the property, each framed by wildflowers. A cool breeze carries their sweet scent through the air.

After checking in, we shed our clothes and are guided behind one of the larger cottages. Water cascades from overhead sprinklers, turning the space into a makeshift rain dance.

People are laughing, spinning, their bodies slick with water as they move to the pulsing flamenco beat. As always, there's no sign of Dove or Julien.

Ava giggles and pulls me in. Everyone is bare and carefree. We greet all the familiar couples from the previous experience and stay dancing until the showers stop.

There's a collective sigh at the interruption, but as we're grabbing towels, someone points out a long circle of small tents set up in the middle of the open grounds. We walk over to find massage tables within each tent, with a blindfolded staffer waiting inside.

Feeling lighter, I place a soft kiss on Ava's cheek and step into the one that has my name outside.

I'm surprised to find a male masseuse beside my table and while my instinct says I ask for an exchange with a female, I decide not to make a fuss and just enjoy the process.

"Hey!" I greet politely, grabbing the gift bag on the side while settling down on the massage table.

"Good evening, Sir. I've been instructed to take my blindfold off only if the client requests.

The man's voice is soft and his manner is detached which immediately puts me at ease. The gift bag has an assortment of exotic edibles along with a silver box with my name on it. My fingers hesitate for a moment before lifting the lid, revealing a diamond-encrusted collar resting on top of velvet casing. My breath catches in my throat.

Below it is a platinum butt plug, a gleaming ruby crowning its end. Holy shit!

My pulse quickens. A flood of memories from the last time we were here hits me. The pegging couple that had indulged with my wife.

But this is more than just sex. It's complete submission. Ownership.

I run my thumb over the card tucked beneath the items, the words igniting a fire in my gut.

"I'm glad my little submissive showed up. Wear my gifts to show I own you. Find me before midnight."

Fuck! It's Dove.

Heat courses through my veins. This isn't just a game anymore. Is this what she wanted all along? Is this why Julien invited us back? Is she pushing the boundaries… or am I?

I fiddle around with the butt plug while my mind races with questions.

I close my eyes, gripping the card tighter, my mind flickering back to Ava with Jax before I remember Dove's whispered plea to Julien: "What if we keep him?"

My body instantly reacts and I find my cock hardening just at the thought of her behind me. Maybe this is what I need. Maybe I've wanted this all along. But how far am I willing to go?

I set the collar and the plug back in the bag, feeling my breath come shorter. This isn't me. At least, that's what I tell myself. But maybe it could be.

My hesitation lingers, the weight of what I'm about to do pressing down on me. Ava wouldn't understand. No one would.

But Dove would. She does.

The masseuse waits. His blindfold still on. "Would you like to start?" His voice is soft and neutral.

I swallow hard, the butt plug is still heavy in my hand. "Ever helped a client with a butt plug?" I ask, my voice lower than intended.

There's a pause. "I have. If you'd like assistance, I'm here to help."

I exhale, a shiver running down my spine as I feel myself edging closer to something I can't fully control. "Fine. Take off the blindfold. Let's start."

Over the next hour and a half, we go through a whole lot inside that tent, and I walk out with the bathrobe to cover my ass and the raging hard-on I'm sporting. The collar is in one of the pockets.

Can't wait to be inside Dove while the plug is inside me—or whatever else she has in mind.

I just need to find her first.

Stepping outside, I find several fire pits lit in the denser part of the property. Music pulsates, drinks are being picked up from the open bar, and people are lounging around.

One particular fire pit has more people around and it's where I find Ava sitting on Butch's lap. One of the guys is telling a story while Butch whispers things in her ear, running his palms all over her.

The rough fingers lingering over her erect nipples till he slyly starts playing with them. He releases one of her nipples to turn her face closer to his before slowly starting to kiss her lips.

The bastard didn't bother with a towel or a robe so I can imagine his cock must be rubbing over her slit raw.

I notice Ava's chest heaving a bit and I realize once again I have an option–walk away again or stay and watch. Or…

"Babe," I say, once I'm a few feet away from them, my mind spinning. Ava disentangles from Butch as soon as she sees me, coming to my side with a smile.

"I was waiting for you," she says, voice soft, as if she hadn't just been grinding against another man.

I loosen my bathrobe, my gaze still fixed on Butch. "On your knees," I command.

Ava's eyes widen for a second before she complies, a smile playing on her lips as she gets to work.

Placing several wet, pouty kisses on the head before running her tongue over it multiple times before slowly starting to suck. Her warm mouth is like a tight cave.

Butch's eyes don't move away from us even for a second.

Soon I'm hitting the back of Ava's throat and I close my eyes, letting the pleasure take over, but all I can picture is Dove. Her voice. Her control.

Ava's moans pull me back, and just as I feel myself on the edge, I yank her head back and finish all over her face, something I've never done in eleven years with her.

Her look of surprise strangely soothes my insides.

She had asked me to let my anger out and today I have. But guilt follows almost immediately.

Grabbing a towel from the side I gently wipe her face before kissing her cheek.

"We're good, but I'm setting you free for these four days. You're free to do whoever and whatever without me. No guilt. No shame. No anger. I promise."

Ava holds on to me tight for a while, her head resting on my chest before I kiss the top of her head and move away.

Getting myself a drink, I stay in a quieter corner, watching people indulge. With each movement, I still feel the butt plug inside me. As the sky gets darker, I start looking around for Dove.

The property is vast, and after a few rounds, I'm ready to give up when I spot a small building hidden behind a waterfall. Not wanting to lose the collar, I wear it and navigate the slippery ropes, determined to find Dove.

My pulse quickens as I manage to cross the waterfall.

Standing on the other side, dressed in a sparkling red dominatrix outfit, is Dove.

Chapter 3: Pushing Boundaries

Ethan

Her perfume hits me before I get close, sending my pulse racing. Her hair is pulled back into a sleek bun, accentuating her sharp jawline.

Her body—God, her body—more toned than I remember, like she's been sculpted from memory but made better. Legs that seem to go on forever, perched in stilettos so high they should be illegal.

And then there's that red leather harness, strapping her like a wild, dangerous present—lush tits exposed, daring me to come closer. My chest tightens.

Sensing my presence, she turns to me, her eyes light up as she surges toward me, wrapping her arms around me, and for a brief moment, it's pure joy.

This is the real Dove. Not the dominatrix. Not the submissive.

And she is genuinely happy to see me again. But she pulls back quickly, her gaze turning sharp and authoritative. Getting into her role I assume.

"Did you use both my gifts?" she demands, her voice sharp.

A jolt of exhilaration shoots through me. I nod, trying to contain my eagerness. Her lips curl into a satisfied smile as she motions me toward a cushioned lounger right in the open, outside the cottage to the side.

"Bend over," she instructs, "I need to check."

My skin zings with excitement and I do exactly as asked.

I drop the bathrobe, crouching over the lounger, my body still damp from the waterfall. I let my eyes dart around, looking for Leon.

"Looking for something?" Dove's sharp voice snaps me back.

I shake my head, struggling to stay composed. She doesn't know I know about her and Leon.

"Spread your legs."

I shudder as her hands slide over my ass, circling slowly, teasing. Her fingers trail down tracing the path on my crack, lingering at the jeweled plug. My breath hitches.

"Good," she whispers, her fingers dipping lower, palming my cock from behind. I buck, a sharp groan escaping as her grip tightens.

"Fuck," I breathe. I'm ready for her to take control.

Out of the corner of my eye, I spot some movement and freeze, expecting it to be Leon, but a striking brunette walks in instead.

What is she here for?

"Lana, fetch the strap-on and fit it on me." Dove's tone is absolute, leaving no room for hesitation and I tighten my grip around the back of the lounger, still crouching over it. Her fingers are still clasped around my length.

Lana is quick to respond and soon Dove moves away from me.

"Get on the lounger," is all she says to me while Lana fits the skin-colored dildo attached to these multiple belts.

I quickly crouch on it, but my eyes stay on the two women. I don't miss the rear end of the dildo that Lana slides inside Dove's glistening slit. So she will feel it as well?

I rub my thighs, swallow a few deep breaths, wondering how painful it would be to take this dildo in. I don't know if I'm ready.

Dove palms the slim dildo, moving it around, checking if its firmly in place before turning to me.

She smirks and smacks my ass hard. "I need you on your back." My eyes widen. What does she have in mind?

In an instant, she lifts one leg, hooking her heel on the edge of the lounger, tilting her head with curiosity before straightening. Leaning in lower, her tits in my face, she grabs my hair, pulling back to stare at me, then pushes the dildo right into my line of sight. My breath hitches.

With her free hand, she rubs the tip against my lips and whispers, "Suck."

My mind immediately goes back to what I had witnessed the last time between her and Julien. He had done the same thing to her. She is now recreating it with me.

Taking another deep breath, I think of it as an extension of Dove and take it in my mouth, grabbing it from the base with my palm.

The taste of strawberries floods my mouth as the tip of the dildo slides past my lips. It surprises me—sweet and oddly comforting, easing some of the tension that's been building in my chest.

Dove's grip tightens in my hair, pulling just enough to remind me of who's in control.

"Good boy," she whispers, her voice dripping with approval. My pulse races faster, and I try to focus on pleasing her, bobbing my head just the way I remember her doing it for Julien. I want to get it right.

Her hand loosens for a moment, and I catch a glimpse of her reaching for something from the small table beside us. The unmistakable flick of a lighter makes my stomach twist in anticipation. The scent of the cigarette slowly filling the air.

I glance up between my head bobs, to see her lips curled around the cigarette, eyes half-lidded, enjoying both the taste of nicotine and the control she holds over me. She exhales slowly, the smoke drifting around her like a veil.

Her free hand moves back to my head, fingers tangling in my hair as she guides me deeper. "Roll your tongue on it and start pushing it up."

I obey immediately and notice her flip a button on the side and the damned thing starts vibrating in my mouth.

She takes another drag, her fingers tightening in my hair, pulling me closer.

"Just like that," she purrs, smoke curling from her lips. '

I push harder with my mouth and she moans.

Before I get lost in the rhythm, Dove's voice cuts through the fog in my mind. "Lana, I want my submissive pleasured."

The command throws me for a loop, but the next moment, I feel hot breath on my cock. My eyes flutter closed as she takes me in, warm and wet. My body reacts instantly, tightening as I fight to keep control, but it's impossible. The sensations of the plug inside my ass, Lana's mouth on my cock and mine pleasuring Dove overwhelm me, and within moments, I reach the edge.

I come hard, biting back a groan, my body shaking with release. Lana swallows it all in and keeps moving till my body relaxes. Dove's grip on my hair loosens slightly as I gasp for air, my mind still reeling from the intensity. Lana's lips leave me, and I sag into the lounger, trying to catch my breath.

Dove chuckles softly, and I open my eyes to find her smirking down at me. "I like how open you are for me, Ethan. You're willing to do whatever I ask, and that's why I reward you."

Her words hit me like a drug, filling me with a heady sense of satisfaction. She strokes my cheek. "And remember, if not Lana, others are willing to please you. All you have to do is follow my orders."

Others? I frown. Who else is around?

Moving her leg away from me, she pulls off the strap-on from around her waist, hands it to Lana, removes her heels, and removes the plug that had been lodged in me all this time. I breathe easy once it's out.

"Come, let's relax now." She extends her palm toward me and I follow her lead. Lana is right behind us.

The breeze around the waterfall is cooler. The sound of the rushing water is soothing, grounding me after the intensity of what just happened.

Dove settles onto a smooth rock by the water's edge, and I sit beside her, my mind still racing. I glance at her, then finally ask what's been sitting heavy on my mind. "What about Julien?"

Her reaction is immediate. Her eyes flare with surprise, then darken with a flash of something sharp.

"You submit to me, Ethan," she says, her voice low. "You follow commands. You don't get to ask questions."

The reprimand is like a slap, and I lower my gaze, swallowing hard. The need to know about Julien gnaws at me.

She soon asks me to go down on her and while I get between her legs, Lana starts fondling and sucking her tits.

I wonder if Dove's assignment this time is to control two people at a time.

"Lana, please leave us," she suddenly announces and my eyes widen. She watches till Lana disappears before urgently grabbing hold of my hand, she races down a path at the other end.

"Where are we going?" I whisper, but she only giggles until we reach a space between two large rocks. It's nearly pitch dark, but she crouches and pushes a smaller rock aside, letting in a flood of light.

She leans into me when I join her, pushing me on my back, her leg circling my waist and her lips meeting mine.

We kiss. Something we haven't done before. At least not like this.

Realization dawns on me: this isn't one of Julien's tests. She's kissing me because she knows no one is watching.

Her lips are like fucking strawberries. Soft, juicy, plump and super sweet. Maybe it's her lip balm.

I pull her closer in my arms, holding her tight and kissing her like she means everything to me. Which in this secluded moment she does.

Between kisses, she murmurs, "I've missed you," and I find my eyes burning. My insides getting heavy.

I don't reply because I don't want her to hear me get vulnerable. So I pull her on top of me and we continue kissing.

The distant sound of loud collective cheers interrupts us and she pulls away.

"It's almost midnight," she murmurs, swiftly getting up. "Let's head back."

Lana is right at the edge of the waterfall, standing sentry till we walk back and the moment she spots us, she races to the cottage.

Strange. I don't comment though.

Once we're inside, Dove goes back to her cold, imposing manner.

"You did well earlier," she murmurs, "But I want to push your boundaries a bit more."

Her hand slides into a drawer, emerging with a new toy—another butt plug. But this one's silicone and seems oversized.

The sight of it sends a jolt through me, a mix of excitement and apprehension.

This one is going to hurt.

"Wait…" I start, but she silences me with a finger on my lips.

"Relax," she soothes. "I'll be with you every step of the way. This is just another way to explore your limits."

Her hands are warm and soothing as she prepares me rubbing lube inside me.

"Focus on my voice," she instructs, her tone both reassuring and authoritative. "You're doing great. Breathe."

As she starts to insert the plug, the stretch makes me flinch. She keeps adding lube, teasing me and slowly I'm able to adjust to the thickness but the sensation is strange and different from the previous one. Dove's voice guides me through it, her praise making each moment a bit easier.

"There we go," she coos. "You're doing so well. I'm proud of you."

The plug settles inside me, a constant, heavy presence. Dove's touch lingers on my shoulder, grounding me.

I twitch my ass, and move my legs around, wanting to see if I can walk around with it inside me.

"Julian won't be here until Sunday, so we can explore without interruptions," she whispers in my ear while Lana is in the bathroom, grabbing paper napkins.

Her words spark a thrill and a hint of anxiety. "What... what will we do until then?" I ask, my voice betraying my nerves.

Dove's smile is both mischievous and affectionate. "Come over early tomorrow."

That's all she says before walking me to the door.

I don't want to leave.

The walk back to my own cottage only has me thinking of everything today.

Tomorrow will come faster if I sleep early.

I arrive back to find the queen-size bed in our room already has two occupants. Ava and a man with a hairy chest.

In the bubble that I am, I shove the man closer to Ava, making space for myself and flopping down on the mattress.

I can't wait for tomorrow.

Chapter 4: Redefining Boundaries

Ethan

I wake up to a warm, wet sensation around my cock. There's a tightness accompanying it. My mind is still hazy with sleep, but the sensation is undeniably pleasurable. I groan in appreciation, instinctively reaching for the familiar curve of Dove's body.

I'm about to whisper her name, pulling her closer but then I hear a groan beside me and open my eyes to find Ava with her head between my legs, her lips wrapped tightly around my cock.

The image feels wrong.

I glance over and see the stranger from last night lounging nearby, watching us with a smirk, rubbing his semi-hard cock.

The sight has me recoiling.

Ava looks up, her eyes sparkling. "I'm so glad you brought us here, babe," she murmurs, releasing me with a pop sound. "I thought I'd wake you up with a surprise."

I'm just waking up, but I know I don't want this.

The hairy chest shifts, his gaze never leaving us. "I'd love to join if you guys are game," he sounds chirpy first thing in the morning. "We have good chemistry, right, Ava?"

I push back, sitting up, propping my back against the headboard. Ava is welcome to him but not me.

Ava shakes her head, smiling at him. "I need a little one-on-one time with my main guy first."

She turns back to me, her fingers tracing along my length, maybe waiting for me to say something but I pointedly stare at the ape till he is out of the room.

"You good?" she asks, slowly proceeding to climb on top of me but I hold her by her waist.

"Wait."

She frowns at me confused and I clear my throat. "We don't have a condom here."

"But it's just us. We never use it."

I shake my head. Not happening. "I'm not even in the mood right now, babe."

I deliberately use her favorite word. 'Babe'.

Her face falls at the blatant rejection since my cock is hard, but after her letting a biker inside her raw, there's no way I'm going there.

Between us, while I've always been the voice of reason, she's the risk-taker. The roles have been stuck. She keeps taking more risks and I try to be logical about them. It's exhausting.

"How about we go have breakfast together? I'm starving."

She agrees and rolls off me, essentially doing what I always do—leave without questioning.

I lock the bathroom door behind me, carefully take the butt plug out of my ass and hide it before going back to my wife.

The breakfast buffet is laid out by a lake at the back of the property. Instead of separate seating like last time, there is one massive community table with benches on either side.

The place is already bustling.

No sign of Dove again but I do notice Lana pouring herself a cup of coffee. Our eyes meet but she looks away as if she doesn't know me. Interesting. I wonder if she is Julian's minion brought over only to keep an eye on his favorite submissive.

"You know her?" Ava asks leaning in closer as we take our seats.

I take a long sip of my iced coffee before turning to her, "Who?"

Ava seems unfazed but changes topic. "How about we play with some other couples today? People think I'm keeping my husband all to myself."

I'd rather not waste time with others when I can have Dove exclusively. Of course, I can't tell my wife that.

"I'm more comfortable exploring individually. I'm not as free as you are."

Ava narrows her eyes, probing. "Who have you been indulging with? I haven't seen you with anyone."

I hesitate. "I don't even know her name."

Ava raises an eyebrow. "So, just one woman? Is it the same one from last time? Is she here?" She scans the room, her expression eager. "Point her out to me."

"She isn't here right now."

Ava's gaze sharpens, her posture stiffening. She knows I'm hiding things. "Remember our agreement, Eth? You can't get emotionally attached to anyone or play with the same person. There's always that risk."

I smirk, leaning back slightly. "Like Marcus? Or that bald guy? Or Jax? You can't reach an orgasm without moaning his name and you're reminding me of rules?"

Ava's eyes flash with anger, her jaw tightening. "It's not the same thing. It was just sex."

Her convenient use of past tense for something she continues doing has me gritting my teeth. I lean forward, voice low but intense. "The rules don't apply differently to you just because you proposed this open marriage. After what happened at home last week, it's best if we forget about rules since you've already broken them all."

We continue our mini-tiff at the community table, some eyes glancing our way, curious whispers filling the air.

"Yeah, but if you're also getting with women, why hide it? And why be angry with me? I don't get it."

I snap, my frustration boiling over. "It's the disrespect. You flaunt your flings in my face all the damn time. You don't even try to hide. It's as if you like to get caught."

"It's how I am. I don't like to hide."

I roll my eyes, exhaling sharply. "Well, I'm private. I intend to keep my shit to myself. You want every last detail?" I take a long pause, watching her. "Well, you're not getting it."

With a swift motion, I push the breakfast tray back, the clatter drawing more eyes on us, and storm away from the gathering. To hell with what others think.

Ava chases after me. She catches up, breathless. "What do you want from me? I just said let's play together. You can keep your private flings to yourself. But you don't even want to be with me now?"

I turn to face her, my frustration boiling over. "The question is: What do you want from me? I told you you're free to do whoever, whatever. Is that not good enough for you now? Do you want me on the floor under your heel, watching you fuck other people?"

This time, she doesn't chase after me.

I take a long, cold shower, trying to clear my head until I remember the silicone butt plug. A strange mix of relief and intrigue washes over me at the thought of ass play. Turning the water warm, I grab some lube from the vanity and explore myself with my fingers, savoring the sensations before reaching for the butt plug.

Crouching, I lube myself thoroughly before slowly pushing it in, groaning as it stretches me. I start to stroke it inside, my cock hardening with each movement.

Slowly, I pull it out, enjoying the flutters it leaves behind.

I don't want to be late for Dove.

Reaching for the collar, I slip it around my neck and stare at myself in the mirror.

I feel different. Like a man who is no longer afraid of boundaries.

Chapter 5: The Edge of Ecstasy

Ethan

The collar presses tight around my neck, a constant reminder of the control I've surrendered to Dove, a sensation that stirs something raw and unfamiliar in me. The plug, snug inside, serves as another silent command, but tonight, it feels heavier.

With Leon returning tomorrow, a strange weight settles in my chest. Is this it? Is this the last time I'll be here with her? The thought gnaws at me, a hollow ache that creeps into my mind, mixing desire with a lingering sense of loss.

Dove isn't by the waterfall or outside on the lounger. I find her in the bathroom, reclining in a clawfoot tub.

A tray rests across the lip, filled with drinks, some food, and a book. She glances up, glasses perched low on her nose, hair in a messy bun, a quiet smirk tugging at the corner of her lips.

Her eyes light up when she sees me, and excitement coursing through me, sharp and immediate.

"I thought you forgot… or maybe decided not to come," she says softly, her smile widening as she sets the book aside.

The air is thick with the scent of her perfume, mingling with the bath oils.

"That wasn't going to happen."

She stares at me for a moment longer than usual before grinning. "I wonder what held you back."

Without another word, she rises from the water, droplets sliding down her skin, leaving it glistening like polished marble. The sight makes my cock strain painfully against the fabric of the bathrobe and I can't tear my eyes away from the way the water clings to her curves as she walks over to me.

As her hands loosen the belt of my robe, a shiver runs down my spine. Her wet body presses against mine, every inch of her skin warm, soft, and intoxicating.

"Wipe me," she whispers, her breath hot against my skin. My hand trembles as I reach for the towel, the simple act somehow loaded with meaning. Does she sense the growing tightness in my chest? The mix of reverence and affection?

I obey, but my mind races, uncertain if this closeness is something I can let go of so easily.

Her nipples harden under my gaze, and I can feel the weight of her body leaning into mine.

"You've taken to the plug so easily," she purrs, her voice thick with amusement as I continue to dry her. Her breath is hot against my neck, her lips grazing the sensitive skin. "I wonder what your kinks are. What have you explored, what have you always wanted to try?"

I hesitate, feeling a pang of embarrassment. Compared to the experiences I've witnessed here, I feel like a bloody novice.

Her fingers distract me, cupping my cock, her thumb gently stroking it. I hold back my moan.

"I haven't done much," I admit as my breath quickens.

"Really? Not even with your wife?"

I shake my head. "Not like this."

She pulls the towel from my hands and tosses it aside, her gaze locking onto mine with a predatory gleam. "Well, let's change that. Tell me what you want," she demands, her fingers sliding over my cock again, this time squeezing, sending a pulse of pleasure through me.

I'm trembling with need, my mind spinning. What do I want? I've always been more of a giver, but with Dove, it's different. I want her to demand things from me.

"I want to please you," I breathe out. "I want to give you something you've never had."

Her eyes darken, a spark igniting. "Really?"

I nod, my heart pounding. "Whatever you want."

Her hands find mine, pulling them behind her to cup her bare ass, the soft warmth of her skin making me ache. She presses her body against mine, the heat of her skin melding with mine.

My cock strains harder as I feel her wet heat so close. "Is that so?" she murmurs, her lips grazing mine.

I nod, breathless.

"Then let's get started," she purrs, her voice sultry and low.

Her mouth is on mine, soft at first, then demanding, her teeth catching my bottom lip as she nips, her tongue slipping inside to taste me. Her breasts pressing into my chest, hips grinding–rubbing the pre-cum from the tip of my cock over her stomach.

"I've never done back-door entry before," she admits, her lips trailing down my neck, her breath hot on my skin. "And I'm not sure my partner would like it."

The way she says partner instead of Julien or her husband doesn't escape me.

"Never had it done to you, or never done it on anyone?" I manage to ask, trying to focus through the haze of desire.

"Both," she says, a flicker of vulnerability crossing her features for the briefest moment before her confidence returns.

I'm on board in nanoseconds. I want to be the first to explore this with her.

"I want to change that," I whisper, pulling her closer.

Her lips curl up as she pushes me back against the wall, her hands roaming my body, igniting every nerve. "Then let's see what you can do."

"Send Lana and him over, please," she commands into the hotel intercom while her eyes stay on me.

Him? Now who is coming? Damnit I can't even ask her. Would he be behind me? In front of me? Or is he being called exclusively for her?

Of all the options, the last one is the one that hurts.

She is the one person, even though forbidden, that I don't want to share.

My mind is still racing when I feel Dove's lips press gently against my shoulder, her breath warm and grounding.

"You okay?"

"I think so," I answer, the thrill outweighing the hesitation.

She kisses me deeply before murmuring against my lips. "We have some time before they get here. Let's take a walk."

We make our way to the waterfall outside and walk along the rocks till she lets her hair down and lowers herself into the stream. Her beautiful naked body still visible under the water. Her pert hips jutting out of the stream as she starts swimming.

I follow, the coolness of the water sharp against the heat still simmering between us. We don't touch. Don't talk. Just swim. Naked. Next to each other.

Lana is outside the cottage when we return, a knowing smile playing on her lips. But the other guy never shows.

"Looks like it's just us," Dove grins at me.

Lana doesn't speak; she quietly watches as Dove leads me to the bed, her hands firm on my shoulders.

"You trust me, right?" Dove's voice is low and I want to tell her 'more than my wife,' instead I whisper, "Of course."

"I'm going to prep you first," she murmurs, her fingers brushing my skin, soothing the storm inside. "Just breathe."

I nod, focusing on my breaths as she slicks the vibrator with lube. The moment she gently pushes it inside me, a wave of sensation crashes over me, both strange and consuming. I can't help but moan; the strange pleasure unfurls inside me.

Dove leaves it vibrating, the sensation intensifying, and lines up in front of me, crouching a bit as Lana lubes her before rolling a condom over my throbbing cock.

The tension shifts, apprehension morphing into pure need as I gently probe her puckered opening. I hesitate, aware that my size might overwhelm her but as I rub the head over her opening, I realize she also has been prepped well.

She takes a deep breath and spreads her legs a bit more and I push forward. Sliding inside with one hard thrust.

"Ahhhhh!"

Her groan sounds a cross between pleasure and pain but my mind is only focused on the snug warmth that envelops me completely.

"God, you feel incredible," I gasp.

"Keep going," Dove urges, her voice thick with desire, pushing me further into uncharted territory.

I tug at her hips, trying to pull her closer as I slowly start thrusting inside her. Her moans urging me to go harder, deeper. I press my palm on her back pushing her face deeper into the mattress, wanting to give her what she wants.

From the corner of my eye, I notice Lana watching us, her lips parted slightly, her fingers trailing over her own skin as she absorbs the scene. I don't miss the strap already mounted on her hips.

"Harder," Dove moans, her voice ragged, and I obey, driving into her with everything I have.

Suddenly I feel the vibrator being slowly pulled out of me and I brace myself.

Not wanting to hurt Dove with sudden movements, I reduce my pace but don't stop. My breath hitches as another round of cold lube is rubbed over my crack, cold, wet fingers slipping inside, driving in and out of me, and suddenly my back is pushed down and an overwhelming fullness presses against me, stretching every inch.

"Fuck!" I whisper almost missing the loud exhale behind me.

My breath hitches further when I see Lana still in her old spot watching us, her eyes a little wider with surprise.

Fuck! It's a man behind me. I just know it. The cock inside feels hard yet soft, like heated silk. Miles apart from a dildo.

The man's arm traces my chest, scraping my nipples and making me moan. Holding my face he gently kisses my neck. His lips wet, soft, thick. My skin scalds everywhere they touch till they reach up to my ear, blowing hot air in before biting the fleshy lobe.

I feel tender in his arms. A strange euphoria growing inside. More so with Dove in front of me.

I'm about to turn when Dove moans, "Faster, Ethan." Her voice is strangled, signaling she is close.

Lana comes over and sits between Dove's legs, stimulating her clit with a bullet-sized vibrator. Her moans getting louder with each second.

I groan as the man starts moving inside me around the same time Dove is starting to clench around my cock.

Suddenly arms tighten around my waist and I hear grunts.

"Ethan, I'm close," Dove cries out and I start thrusting harder, wanting her to cum to my cock unlike all the other times.

In split seconds, her body freezes and I can feel the intensity of the orgasm ripping through her as her muscles choke my cock, her body trembling against mine.

I continue thrusting in her, keeping pace with the man behind me till Dove slowly moves away.

Just as she does, the thrusts behind me get harder. One of his arms wraps around my waist like vice and the other grabs hold of my cock.

My senses feel overwhelmed.

I had only ever heard of being possessed but for the first time, I experience it.

I throw my head back knowing I'm close and everything fades away except the man moving inside me and his loud grunts and suddenly I see stars.

He finishes right alongside me and we stay locked in an embrace for a while till he slips out of me.

My breath comes in ragged gasps, my body limp, sated, the afterglow pulling me under like a warm tide.

But the ground slips away from under me as I turn, my heart stalling.

Leon D'Armonde–the man behind me, the one who held me so intimately.

My mind reels, struggling to catch up. The shock spreads through me like ice, freezing me in place. How could I not have known? And yet... as his eyes meet mine, smoldering with intensity, something stirs inside me—a mixture of disbelief, confusion, and a terrifying thrill.

What does this mean?

A smirk is playing on his lips when he reaches out to curl his finger around the hook of my collar and pulls my face closer to his.

Our gaze locking. His hot breath on my face. His lips brushing mine. Slowly he leans in and closes the gap.

My lips feel like they are on fire as he kisses me deeply and passionately. His tongue clashing with mine. A taste of peppermint on him.

I'm still grappling with my emotions and the sensations when he pulls away, chuckling.

"I knew we'd be good together the first time I saw you but I didn't know this good."

He wanted me the first time we met? I don't know what to believe anymore.

THE END

Dear reader,

Thank you for reading to the end! I hope the book lived up to your expectations!

Would you like to read more cuckold short stories? If so, check out my Hooked by the BBC series!

Exclusive erotic short story club
Want even more? You can join my exclusive erotic short club **for free**. By doing so, you will get a bunch of free stories (before I publish

them), audiobook coupon codes, and much more! Email me at amber.carden.books@gmail.com and I will send you a link!

Amber

© Copyright 2024 - All rights reserved.

The content contained within this book may not be reproduced, duplicated, or transmitted without direct written permission from the author or the publisher.

This book is copyright protected. It is only for personal use. You cannot amend, distribute, sell, use, quote or paraphrase any part, or the content within this book, without the consent of the author or publisher.

www.ingramcontent.com/pod-product-compliance
Lightning Source LLC
LaVergne TN
LVHW041630070526
838199LV00052B/3305